GREAT BUDDHIST STORIES

STORIES the BUDDHA TOLD

S. DHAMMIKA
&
SUSAN HARMER

TIMES BOOKS INTERNATIONAL
Singapore • Kuala Lumpur

Ven. S. Dhammika was born in Australia in 1951. He was ordained as a Buddhist monk in India and later lived in Sri Lanka where he became well known for his efforts to promote Buddhism. In 1985, he moved to Singapore to become spiritual advisor to the Buddha Dhamma Mandala Society, a post he held until 1992 when he returned to Sri Lanka. Ven. Dhammika has written numerous books and made several television films on Buddhism.

Susan Harmer was born in Singapore in 1955. She taught music in England for many years before returning to Singapore in 1989 to embark on a career as an illustrator. Since then, she has worked extensively in both advertising and publishing. She now spends her time equally between teaching music and illustrating books. Her keen interest in Buddhism has led her to collaborate with Ven. Dhammika on *Great Buddhist Stories*.

STORIES the BUDDHA TOLD

Text by Valerie Hutapea

Special thanks to Hutapea Hasudungan

© 2001 Ven. S. Dhammika and Susan Harmer

Published by Times Books International
An imprint of Times Media Private Limited
A member of the Times Publishing Group
Times Centre
1 New Industrial Road
Singapore 536196
Tel: (65) 2848844 Fax: (65) 2854871
E-mail: tedcsd@tpl.com.sg
Online Book Store: http://www.timesone.com.sg/te

Times Subang
Lot 46, Subang Hi-Tech Industrial Park
Batu Tiga
40000 Shah Alam
Selangor Darul Ehsan
Malaysia
Tel & Fax: (603) 7363517
E-mail: cchong@tpg.com.my

Printed in Malaysia

ISBN 981 232 181 0

CONTENTS

The Persevering Quail

Once, in a forest near Benares, there lived a quail.

I'd better get out of the way before that lightning strikes me.

BROOM

Suddenly...

CRACK

Oh no!

If that fire's not put out, all the animals in the forest will be killed. I must do something.

Again and again, she sprinkled water on the fire.

Suddenly...

CRASH

It's no use! The fire seems to be getting bigger.

But I can't stop. I must keep trying.

Meanwhile, the gods in heaven were watching.

Look at what's happening down there.

What a foolish bird. She's not trying to put the fire out all by herself, is she?

She'll never do it. She might as well give up now.

Tell her to stop what she's doing and save herself.

All right...

...but I'll turn myself into an eagle first.

5

The fire's worse than I thought.

I can hardly see her with all this smoke.

Little quail, little quail!

Don't talk to me. Can't you see I'm busy?

You won't put the fire out like that.

Escape and save yourself while you can.

Friend, I don't need your advice. I need your help.

But...

I'm not leaving! So you can either stay and give me a hand, or go!

What determination!

Well?

She won't listen to me. She's determined to keep going.

Perhaps we ought to help her.

You're right. She seems such a brave little bird.

Let's make it rain.

May the heavens open up!

And so it began to rain...

...and rain...

...and rain...

...until at last, the fire went out.

Whew! That was hard work but I knew I could do it!

We should reward the little bird for her efforts.

Yes, let's give her something beautiful so that everyone will remember her perseverance.

And so this is how quails came to have crowns on their heads.

The End

THE PROUD ASCETIC

Once, in the city of Benares, there lived an ascetic.

Although he had renounced the world, he was proud and vain.

Magnificent!

If that isn't the reflection of the holiest man in India, then I don't know what is!

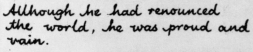

Now it's off to meet my public.

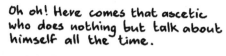
Ah, I see a group of people ahead. I'll stop and give them the benefit of my knowledge.

Oh oh! Here comes that ascetic who does nothing but talk about himself all the time.

Once he starts, there's no stopping him.

Let's get out of here.

They're moving away. They can't have seen me.

Hello there, good people!

Too late!

Would you like me to tell you about my meditation attainments?

Sorry, can't stay. We're in a hurry.

Hummph...

Well, it's their loss, not mine.

They don't know a saint when they see one.

MAHOSADHA'S TESTS

Once, in the royal palace in Mithila...

There is a prophecy that a child of great wisdom has been born in this city.

As my Four Wise Men what do you think of this?

Who made this silly prophecy, sire?

You did, Senaka, about seven years ago.

I did?

Then it must be true.

Sire, there's a child living near the Eastern Gate of the city who's supposed to be remarkably clever.

How old is this child?

About seven.

That must be him.

I'll send someone to investigate the matter and if he is the child, he will become one of my advisors.

But sire, you already have the four of us. Why do you want another?

Because five heads are better than four!

Chamberlain! Go to the Eastern Gate. Observe carefully what goes on and then report back to me.

A little later...
Now look what you've done.

That little upstart might end up outshining us.

We'd better think of something fast.
That won't be easy.

Later, at the Eastern gate...
Perfect! I can see everything for miles around from up here.

Hey, give me back my cotton!

It's mine!
No, it's not! I made it! It's mine!

Liar!
How dare you call me a liar!

Someone call Mahosadha. We'll soon find out who's telling the truth.

Minutes later...
Mahosadha, how are you going to settle this problem?
Easy. Leave it to me.

I'll take that if you don't mind.

When you make a ball of cotton, you have to begin by winding it around something.

What did you use?

I...er...used a stick.

And you?

I used a cotton seed.

Now let's unwind the ball.

A cotton seed!

All right! I admit I took it.

I'm sorry, I'm sorry, I'll never do such a thing again.

Not bad for a youngster. Let's see what else he can do.

Just then, not far away...

Oooh! What have we here? The perfect goblin supper — a nice fat baby!

WAAA

The mother's bound to have heard that. Noisy brat!

I was right. She's coming back. Curses!

I'll have to change into a disguise.

This will fool anyone.

What's the matter, dearest? Why were you crying?

Hello there!

Huh!

You startled me!

Oh, what a lovely baby.

I'll have him. He's so cute!

What...?!!

You know what they say—finders keepers! Goodbye!

No!

My baby! Come back with my baby!

At the Eastern Gate...

I can hardly believe my eyes. That poor woman.

But wait! Here comes Mahosadha.

Help me, please!

What's wrong?

That woman! She stole my baby. Stop her!

Let me go! I've done nothing wrong.

Give me back my baby!

The woman's mad. This child belongs to me.

Mahosadha, you're so clever at deciding such things. Who is the true mother?

Mmh... this tree stump is ideal.

Bring the child here.

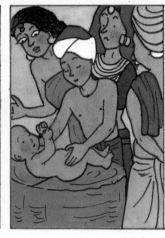

Now you take the arms...

... and you take the legs.

Whoever can pull the child across the line I've drawn is the baby's true mother.

This shouldn't be too difficult.

One...two... three...

...pull!

Oh, my poor baby! I can't hurt him like this! I must let go!

WAAAA

17

I've seen enough!

Time to report back to the King.

Later...

And so, for the second time, Mahosadha came to the rescue.

A remarkable child indeed! Chamberlain,...

...go and invite him to join the Court as one of my Wise Men.

For goodness sake, do something, Senaka!

Wait, Your Majesty! Solving those problems doesn't prove he's wise.

Quite right!

What do you mean?

Yes, what do you mean?

Those were just common, everyday problems. Anyone could have solved them. If he is really wise...

...then he should be able to pass a test that we ourselves set for him.

Well... all right! What test do you have in mind?

Leave it to us, Your Majesty. We'll think of something.

Good work, Senaka.

Be quiet! I have to think!

Later...

But this is impossible. No one could solve this problem.

If he's really wise, it should be easy for him.

Very well, Chamberlain. Read this proclamation to the people at the Eastern Gate.

Early the next morning...

The King demands that you send him a bull that is white...

...with a hump on his head and horns on his legs.

If it cannot be done, you will be punished.

Where can we get such a creature?

Does it even exist?

Mahosadha, what are you doing? This is no time to play. We need your help.

SQUAWK

20

We'll send the King a rooster.

A rooster? But he wants a bull!

Well, a rooster is male like a bull. It is also white,...

...it has a "hump" on its head...

...and "horns" on its legs.

Brilliant!

Later...

A very ingenious solution to your problem, Senaka.

I will appoint Mahosadha to the court immediately.

Oooh, you disgusting animal!

Wait, Your Majesty!

Let us give him one more test.

Please, Sire!

Oh, very well! But only one more. If he passes this time...

...he shall become one of my Wise Men.

Soon after...

He won't outsmart me again. I'll make sure of that.

Much later...

I've got it!

The next day...

The King has a swing with ropes made of sand. These ropes are now broken. Provide him with new ones...

...or you will all be punished.

Back at the village...

A rope made out of sand?

Whoever heard of such a thing? What are we to do?

Mahosadha thought hard...

Where are you going?

To see the King.

We're coming too!

22

What do you think he's going to do?

At the palace...

So this is Mahosadha. He doesn't look very impressive.

Majesty, we have not brought you new ropes because we do not know how thick they should be.

He's trying to wriggle out of it.

We've got him this time.

But if you would give us a section of the old rope, we will get you a new one of the same thickness.

...er... I do not have such ropes.

Well, if Your Majesty hasn't got any, how can simple folk like us get some?

Ha, ha! Well done! You have been tested enough.

I hereby proclaim you one of my Wise Men!

LONG LIVE MAHOSADHA

Senaka, does this mean we're not so wise after all?

OH BE QUIET!

The End

23

THE FIVE WISE MEN

One day, by the Royal Kitchen in Mithila...

I haven't eaten for days.

sniff sniff

Oh, that does smell good!

The cook's not looking. Here's my chance.

What the...?

I'll teach you a lesson.

Yelp!

And I don't want to see you hanging around here anymore, understand?

Meanwhile, in the Royal Stables...

Those leaves look good!

That's not for you. Go on, get out!

And don't come back again!

Owww!

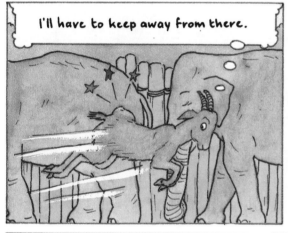

I'll have to keep away from there.

CRASH

Looks like he's been beaten.

What happened to you?

sniff sniff

Trouble in the stables. And you?

Trouble in the kitchen.

25

I think we have the same problem.

You're hungry too, aren't you?

Yes, but maybe we can work together and find a solution.

How?

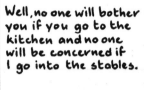

Well, no one will bother you if you go to the kitchen and no one will be concerned if I go into the stables.

Oh, I see! Then I can get meat for you...

...and I can get leaves for you.

Let's try it!

Later in the kitchen...

What was that? If it's that pesky dog again, I'll...

...oh, it's only a goat. The meat'll be safe.

I'll wait till he goes.

Meanwhile at the stables...

Hello, old fellow.

26

What are you doing here?

Nice to have a dog around.

He's not looking. I'll just grab a mouthful of leaves and be off.

Soon afterwards...

MUNCH MUNCH MUNCH MUNCH

Don't you think this is a good arrangement?

Burrrp!

HA HA HA HA HA

One day, the King was on the palace wall...

That's something you don't see everyday. Dogs and goats usually fight with each other.

I wonder how they became friends.

The King watched and saw how they helped each other...

So that's it!

I have Five Wise Men. I'll test them to see if they're worth their high wages.

The next day...

By the palace wall are a dog and a goat—two natural enemies living as friends.

Tell me by tomorrow how this unusual relationship has come about...

...or you will all lose your jobs!

Soon afterwards...

Now we're in trouble.

What are we going to do?

Well, first we ought to go and look at these animals.

I was just about to suggest that.

Later...

There they are. They look the best of friends.

I've never seen such a thing! Why aren't they fighting?

Most strange.

Go closer and see what's unusual about them.

Stop pushing!

WOOF WOOF WOOF

28

Run for your life!

Thank goodness they're not following us.

Pull yourselves together!

What a useless bunch!

Come on! I've got a book on goats. We'd better go and look it up. We've only got till tomorrow.

That's a much safer idea. Wait for us!

I'm going back to the Palace to talk to the Chamberlain.

At the Palace...

You want to know what the King does?

Well, lately he's taken to walking on the top of the West Wall of the Palace.

Shortly afterwards...

I thought so. I can see the two animals clearly from here.

I'll watch for a while and see what happens.

After some time...

So that's it!

Late that night...

Come up with anything yet?

No, how about you?

29

30

Well, we're waiting!

I know what I can do to save us all and still teach these Wise Men a lesson.

I'll write it down for you.

This doesn't make sense.

Is this a trick?

Yes it is, but if you want to keep your jobs...

...you'd better recite it to the King tomorrow and hope he doesn't ask you what it means.

See you in the morning.

The next day...

Well, have you solved the problem?

Sire, we've decided to present you the answer in the form of a poem.

Let me see...

"Stable and Kitchen, Both get a beating, Exchange one for the other, Now both are eating."

We...er...hope that makes sense to you.

Yes, because it doesn't to us!

Congratulations! You have solved the problem!

Oh thank goodness for that!

THE FOOLISH MAGICIAN

Once, there was a young man training to be a magician.

That's the end of the course. You have only one thing left to learn.

At last I'm going to be a proper magician.

I will teach you a spell that can bring the dead back to life.

Oh, good! I'll really impress people with a spell like that.

Now watch carefully and remember what I say.

One, two,
Three, four, five,
Dead thing come alive.

That seems easy enough.

Now you try it on that dead bird.

One,
Two,
Three, four, five,
Dead thing come alive.

Tweet
Tweet

I did it! It's alive again!

Now your studies are finished.

Thank you, Master.

Goodbye but be careful how you use your powers.

Don't worry, I will.

I'm so excited I can't wait to try out what I know.

Sometime later...

I'll go and talk to those people. Perhaps they would like to see me do some magic.

Hello there, strangers. May I join you?

Suit yourself.

I'm a magician, you know.

Perhaps they didn't hear me.

I said I'm a magician! I can do magic.

Would you like me to show you?

Look, we've just come back from hunting and we're very tired.

The last thing we want is to watch a youngster like you perform silly tricks.

How dare you talk to me like that? I'm a fully-qualified magician...

...and my magic is so powerful that I can...

I can...

...I can even bring dead things back to life!

Now what do you say to that?

Care for a hot drink?

Don't you believe me? I can really do it!

HA HA HA

No, you can't!

I can! I can! I CAN!

All right then. There's a dead tiger over there. We killed it today.

Go and bring it back to life. Ha, ha!

I'll show them!

THE CUNNING JACKAL

Once, there was a jackal who lived by the river.

I'm hungry. I'd really love a nice, tasty rohita fish for my supper.

I'll see if I can catch one.

Meanwhile, a little further down the river, there lived two otters.

I see a fish!

You go after him and I'll get him as he comes around that rock.

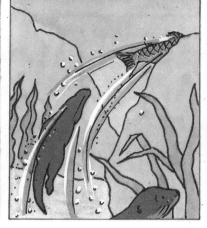

Got you!

You always take the bigger piece!

No, I don't. You do!

What a big, fat fish!

Perhaps I can take advantage of their fighting.

Friends. What seems to be the matter? I can hear you halfway up the river.

We can't agree on how to divide this fish between us.

Then why not let me decide for you?

Well... alright.

Good. Now first of all, tell me what happened.

Well, First I... ...round the rock... he... I never...

No, no, no... it was like this... he really did... I wouldn't...

BLAH! BLAH! BLAH!

Stop! I've heard enough!

It's not going to be an easy case to solve but I will do my best.

Pass me the knife.

Now, you said... and he said...

Yes, I think I have the best solution.

I bet he gets the tail.

What's he doing?

Here, you take this.

And you take this.

But what about the rest of the fish?

That's my fee!

The End

THE PIECE OF STRAW

Once, in a village in Benares, there lived an ascetic.

No work, good food — it's great being an ascetic.

Oh oh! Here comes one of my supporters. I'd better pretend to be meditating.

Everytime I come, I find him meditating. What a model of goodness.

I'll just sit here and wait for him to finish.

As the minutes passed...

I can't sit here like this much longer.

My knees are aching. I must get up. How do these people do it? Oooh... ouch...

41

Venerable sir, forgive me for interrupting your meditation.

Not at all.

I have come to seek your blessings and ask for your help.

You have my blessings. Now just tell me what I can do for you.

I have 100 gold pieces in this bag...

Did he say 'gold'?

... and I'm frightened that burglars might break into my house and steal it.

Can I leave it with you for safekeeping?

Certainly!

No one would think of looking for it here and you're so holy, I know I can trust you to take care of it for me.

Uh!

Ahem! Yes, I am completely free from greed. Your money is safe with me.

Oh thank you, venerable sir.

No, no, it is I who should thank you!

No more grass huts for me. At last I can go back to the city and live in the lap of luxury. I can just see it – a rooftop apartment, wild parties, fast chariots ...

Now I must be off.

Yes, yes, yes. Go in peace.

Soon...

Benares here I come!

Just a minute. If I leave straight away he might get suspicious and come after me.

Better to wait a few days and then disappear with the gold.

In the meantime, I'll bury it to keep it safe. This looks like a good spot.

You can't be too careful. There are lots of thieves about these days.

A few days later...

Now just to make sure he never suspects me, I'll go and tell him I'm leaving.

Soon...

So it might only be for a short while. In any case, I'll see you on my return.

Have a pleasant journey, venerable sir.

So that's the man my father thinks is such a saint.

I'll walk a little way before I go back.

This will fool him.

A short while later...

Venerable sir, why have you returned?

I noticed a piece of straw had fallen into my hair.

It must have come from your roof so I just had to return it to you.

I'd hate you to think I would take something that wasn't mine.

Now I'll be off.

How holy!

How phoney!

What do you mean?

Father, people who are really holy don't make a big fuss over such small things.

I tell you, this ascetic is up to no good. Have you ever given him anything of value?

Why yes. He is looking after 100 gold pieces for me.

But I can't imagine that he would take it.

Oh, father!

Come with me.

Where are we going?

I think he went this way. Let's hurry.

What are we doing here?

Shhh! Get down!

44

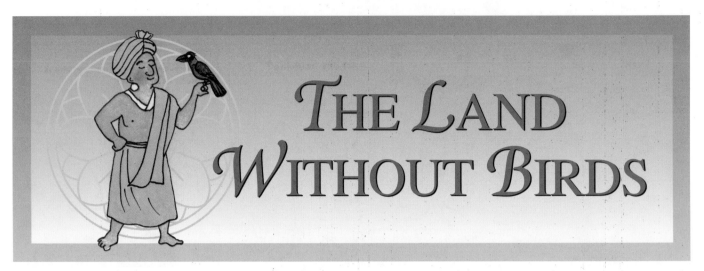

THE LAND WITHOUT BIRDS

Once, a group of merchants set out on a journey...

Have we got everything?

Yes, sir!

Excellent! We should make a small fortune if we sell all our goods.

Untie the ropes! Let down the sails!

Look! That old crow has been with us since we set sail.

He must be hungry. Throw him some scraps.

After a month's sailing, the ship arrived in Bavaru, a barren land with no trees and no birds.

Set up the merchandise right here on the dock.

Soon a crowd gathered...

Indian nutmeg, fresh Indian nutmeg.

Nutmeg? What's that?

It's an Indian spice, sir, and at one gold piece for a 100, I'm practically giving them away.

No thanks, we have something similar here.

Then can I interest you in some cotton cloth?

This is the finest weave in Musilipatanam.

It's a bargain at three gold pieces for one measure.

49

And all because of a bird! Ha! Ha! Ha!

HA HA HA

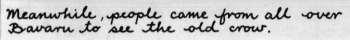

Meanwhile, people came from all over Bavaru to see the old crow.

Isn't it magnificent?

The heavens be praised!

Bring more fruit. He's still hungry.

The following year...

We're going to Bavaru again? And I suppose we're taking a cageful of crows?

No, I've got a better idea. Listen...

That's brilliant! We'll make twice as much profit than last time.

A few weeks later in Bavaru...

Gather round, my friends, gather round.

It's those Indian merchants again

Did you bring another flying creature?

Certainly not! I've got something more interesting than that.

50

The Student Who Could Not Steal

Once, in Taxila, there was a famous teacher.

That's all for today.

Your drink, father.

Thank you, daughter.

It's time she was married.

I would like her to marry one of my students...

... but which one should I choose? They are all handsome and clever...

...but that is not enough. It is much more important to be virtuous.

So how can I tell which one is really good at heart and therefore worthy of my daughter's hand?

I think I have it..

Later that day...

I have decided that my daughter shall marry one of you.

What an honour!

Who is it to be, Master?

I don't know yet...

...but he will need a lot of jewellery for the wedding. As a poor man, I have none to give my dear daughter.

Therefore, the one who can give her the most jewellery shall marry her.

But Master we are poor too. How are we to get jewellery?

I don't mind how or where you get it.

You can even steal it if you like...

...just as long as no one knows that you have been stealing.

Sounds good to me.

I'm not sure about this. We're not thieves.

But how else are we going to get jewellery?

The Master himself said it was OK to steal so I suppose it must be.

Then what are we waiting for? Let's go!

Soon, the crime rate in the nearby villages went up at an alarming rate.

Hand over your jewellery!

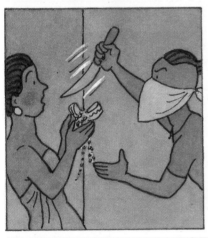

This is fun!

But there was one student who felt differently.

Surely our Master can't mean what he says.

It can never be right to steal — for any reason!

Sometime later...

Well, have any of you managed to get some jewellery?

Oh yes Master!

My teachings have not been in vain.

Make sure every piece of stolen jewellery is returned to their rightful owner.

As for you, you have proved to be the wisest and most virtuous of all my students.

And so you shall marry my daughter.

The couple was married and lived happily ever after.

The End

THE MARK OF GREATNESS

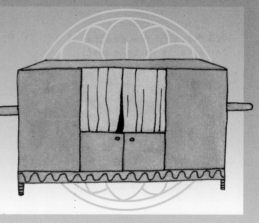

One day, King Mallika was out for a ride.

ZZZZ

King Brahmadatta was also out for a ride.

ZZZZ

They came to a narrow bridge.

Hey, watch out!

What the ...?

Out of the way!

No, you get out of the way!

Why have we stopped?

I'll have you know that King Mallika of Kosala is in this palanquin. Now let us pass.

Well, King Brahmadatta of Benares is in this one.

ZZZZ

Mmmh... this is a deadlock. What can we do?

I know. Whoever we decide is the greater king shall pass first.

It's a deal.

This should prove interesting. I'll listen to what they have to say.

Let's go by age. Whoever is the older gets to cross first.

Fine. King Mallika is 40 years old.

Mmh... so is King Brahmadatta.

We must think of something else.

King Mallika's realm is 1000 leagues around. Beat that!

A fair size even if I say so myself. I'm sure to be the winner.

King Brahmadatta's realm is also 1000 leagues around.

Then how about this — there are no less than 15,000 men in King Mallika's army.

That's nothing to brag about. King Brahmadatta has the same number of men in his army.

Dear me...

All right then. King Mallika is the greater and more powerful king because to those who are kind and fair, he is also kind and fair. But to those who are cruel and harsh...

...he shows no mercy whatsoever!

And quite right too. Return good with good and evil with evil. That's what I always say.

Well, it doesn't matter to King Brahmadatta what people are like. He is kind, fair AND just to everyone he meets.

Without exception!

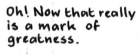
Oh! Now that really is a mark of greatness.

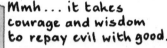
Mmh... it takes courage and wisdom to repay evil with good.

Servant! I overheard everything. Let King Brahmadatta pass!

With pleasure, sire.

Back up!

Thank you

Praise to you, Brahmadatta, and may your journey be safe!

ZZZZ

The End

59

THE TALKATIVE TORTOISE

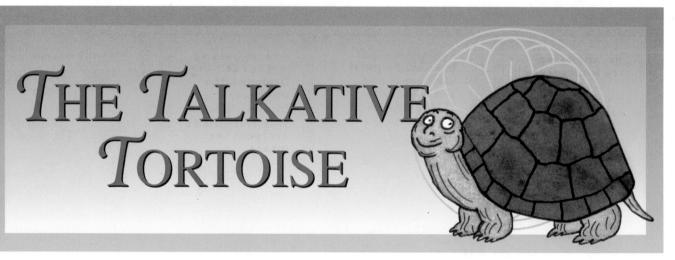

Once, by a pond in the forest...

...so I said to him, I said, this pond here is not your average pond...

...oh no, I said... and I'm not your average tortoise either... no indeed... blah blah blah...

Boy, can he talk!

Mark my words, it'll be the death of him one day.

And not a moment too soon!

...anyhow, he said... blah blah blah...

...blah blah blah...

Excuse me for interrupting but why don't you go and talk to those two geese who have just flown in?

I'm sure they'd love to talk to you.

Hee hee hee!

But I'm only halfway through my story.

No problem! We'll hear the rest of it later! Bye!

Mmmh...those geese seem to be new here. I suppose it's only right that I greet them and say a few words.

Hello there! Welcome to our pond. Not seen you around before. Please make yourselves at home.

Why, thank you!

Whereabouts do you come from? Perhaps I know it. There aren't many places I don't know about. Why only the other day... ...blah blah blah... Can you believe that? Blah...blah...blah...

Ahem! We come from a beautiful lake in the Himalayas where the...

The Himalayas, eh? They're mountains, aren't they? I just love mountains.

Of course I've never seen any. We don't have them around here.

Well, we do actually, but they're more like hills really. No, it'd be nice to see proper mountains. Big, are they? Talking of big... blah blah blah ...blah blah...

Why don't you visit us and see for yourself?

Oh, no! With him around we'd never get a moment's peace.

Well, you know, I'd love to come but it would take me so long to get there. We tortoises are very slow walkers.

Thank goodness for that!

Mind you, if you could think of a way to get me there fast, I wouldn't say no.

We could carry you.

How?

Well, you could hold on to a stick and we could carry it in our beaks.

What a good idea!

What a terrible idea!

I'll try anything once. Do you know, there was a time when I...blah blah...

But you'll have to keep your mouth shut for the entire journey.

Well, I can do that. I can keep my mouth shut - no problem! In fact, I've been told to keep my mouth shut many times before and I've always managed to do it.

You know, never a day passes when someone doesn't tell me to...

Oh, just put this in your mouth!

...kmbjlz!

Now don't forget. Not a word!

Soon...

And we're off!

Oooh! This is so exciting!

62

I bet I'm the world's first flying tortoise. What a story this will make!

This is marvellous! Wait till I tell my relatives back home about this.

They're always complaining that I can't stop talking... well, this will show them.

Nothing will get me to open my mouth. No, indeed. They won't get a word out of me.

Meanwhile, down on the ground...

Will you look at that?

Those people below are looking at me.

I bet they've never seen a flying tortoise before.

Two geese carrying a tortoise! Amazing!

I've never seen a flying tortoise before, have you?

What did I tell you?

Don't be silly. It's just a bunch of old leaves on a stick.

You're probably right. Whoever heard of a flying tortoise? What a ridiculous idea!

Bunch of old leaves...? How dare you? I'm a tortoise - do do hear me?

I SAID I'M A TOR...

63